Limerick County Library

30012 00698451 1

KU-081-272

For my babies, Isobel and Tom D.B.

To my baby, Freddie R.B.

EGMONT

We bring stories to life

First published in Great Britain 2011
by Egmont UK Limited
239 Kensington High Street
London W8 6SA

Text copyright © David Bedford 2011
Illustrations copyright © Rosalind Beardshaw 2011

David Bedford and Rosalind Beardshaw have asserted their moral rights.

ISBN 978 14052 5417 5 (Hardback)
ISBN 978 14052 5418 2 (Paperback)

1 3 5 7 9 10 8 6 4 2

A CIP catalogue record for this title is available from the British Library

Printed and bound in Singapore

All rights reserved. No part of this publication may be reproduced, stored in a retrieval system,
or transmitted, in any form or by any means, electronic, mechanical, photocopying, recording
or otherwise, without the prior permission of the publisher and copyright owner.

Babies

Limerick County Library
00698451

WITHDRAWN FROM STOCK

David Bedford * Rosalind Beardshaw

EGMONT

One warm, sunny day,
Morris found Mini clearing out their molehill.

Limerick
County Library

Morris the mole loved babies.

"**Yippee!**" he said,

"We need to make more room," said Mini. "Our babies are coming soon!"

and he hurried down from the hill to get ready.

The farmyard was full of **happy** babies.

Morris wanted to make his babies happy too.

But how?
Morris looked
more closely and saw . . .

Bunnies.

Hoppy, floppy bunnies.

Morris watched the hoppy, floppy bunnies *hopping* in the field with their dad.

The bunnies were **happy**.

"Hoppy babies are **happy** babies," said Morris,

and he began hopping too

so that he could learn how.

But it wasn't long before . . .

Morris hopped too high!

He landed on his nose.
"Ouch!"

"Are you all right, Morris?" called Mini, from the top of the molehill.

"I think so," said Morris, rubbing his nose.

"Good," said Mini, "because our babies are on their way!"

"**Yippee!**" said Morris, and he hurried off again to get ready.

This time he saw . . .

Chicks.

Chirpy,
chirpy
chicks.

Morris watched the chirpy, chirpy chicks
flapping on the nest with their dad.

The chicks were **happy**.

"Flappy babies
are **happy** babies,"
said Morris,

and he began
flapping too

so that he could
learn how.

But it wasn't long before . . .

Morris **flapped** and **flopped** off the branch!

He tumbled to the ground
and landed on his head.

"Ouch!"

"Are you all right, Morris?"
called Mini, from the
top of the molehill.

"Good," said Mini, "because our babies are nearly here!"

"I think so," said Morris, rubbing his head.

"Yippee!" said Morris, and he hurried off once more to get ready.

This time he saw . . .

Ducklings.

Quacky, quacky ducklings.

Morris watched the quacky, quacky ducklings *splashing* in the pond with their dad.

The ducklings were **happy**.

"Splashy babies are **happy** babies," said Morris,

and he began splashing too
so that he could learn how.

But it wasn't long before . . .

Morris slipped and sploshed into the water!

He landed on his bottom. **"Ouch!"**

Morris waited for Mini to ask if he was all right,

but Mini was nowhere

to be seen.

Morris walked slowly back to
his molehill and sat down.

"My babies are coming
and I am **not** ready,"
he said to himself.

Then a voice from deep inside
the molehill said,

"Hopping makes happy babies.

Flapping makes happy babies.

And splashing makes happy babies.

But I cannot do ANY of those things."

"Our babies
don't NEED
any of
those things,
Morris!"

"Our babies only need . . .

The mole babies kissed and cuddled with their *dad*.
Morris, Mini and their babies were **happy!**

And for ever after that . . .

"Love makes happy babies!" said Morris.

And he gave his babies
all the love they would ever need.

Limerick
County Library
0064845l